ONCE UPON A **TIME,** THE END

Once upon a time, the End

(asleep in 60 seconds)

by Geoffrey Kloske

and

Barry Blitt

ATHENEUM BOOKS FOR YOUNG READERS

NEW YORK   LONDON   TORONTO   SYDNEY

To Courtney, Madelyn, and Alexa —G. K.

To my boy, Sam —B. B.

Atheneum Books for Young Readers

An imprint of Simon & Schuster Children's Publishing Division

1230 Avenue of the Americas, New York, New York 10020

Text copyright © 2005 by Geoffrey Kloske

Illustrations copyright © 2005 by Barry Blitt

Book design by Ann Bobco

The text for this book is set in Golden Cockerel.

The illustrations for this book are rendered in ink and watercolor.

Manufactured in China

8   10   9   7

Library of Congress Cataloging-in-Publication Data

Kloske, Geoffrey.

Once upon a time, the end : asleep in 60 seconds / Geoffrey Kloske ; illustrated by Barry Blitt.— 1st ed.

p. cm.

Summary: A tired father takes only a few sentences to tell a number of classic tales in order to get the persistent listener to fall asleep.

ISBN 0-689-86619-4 (ISBN-13: 978-0-689-86619-7)

[1. Bedtime—Fiction. 2. Characters in literature—Fiction.] I. Blitt, Barry, ill. II. Title.

PZ8.K736On 2005

[398.2]—dc22

2004025756

contents

Once upon a time . . .   1

CHICKEN LITTLE   5

THE TWO LITTLE PIGS   7

SMALL GIRL, RED HOOD   8

GOLDILOCKS AND THE BEARS   11

PRINCESS PEA   12

THE LITTLE RED HEN   14

But in that peaceful little house . . .   15

DAVID AND GOLIATH   18

SLEEPING BEAUTY   19

JACK   20

HICKORY, DICKORY, DOCK   22

JOHN JACOB   22

THE OLD LADY'S SHOE   23

HEY DIDDLE DIDDLE   24

RIDDLE ONE   25

RIDDLE TWO   25

And they all lived . . .   26

Once upon a time
And a long, long time ago,
Late at night
When it was dark,
Over the hills,
Through the woods,
Across a great ocean,
In a land far away,
In a small house,
On a hill,
Under a full moon...

In a big fluffy bed,
Under the covers,
There was a little girl,
Or maybe it was a boy,
Who WOULDN'T go to bed.
"Just one more story," this child cried
Over and over again.
So the noble and tired father obliged,
But as he read,
He started cutting
Little words here and there
So the stories would go faster,
And faster,
And faster,
Until finally his child would be asleep.
And everyone could live happily ever after.
The end.

CHICKEN LITTLE

An acorn hit Chicken Little on the head.
"The sky is falling," she said;
"I must go tell the king."
On the way she ran into his friends:
Zeus the Goose,
Jen the Hen,
Chuck the Duck,
Legal, an eagle,
Perky, a turkey,
And Yo the Crow.
"Let's go tell the king," they cried.
Unfortunately, they ran into a hungry fox.
He chased them around the barnyard
Until Chicken Little was simply too tired to speak.
And so she forgot about the sky,
And the king,
And put her feathered head down,
To sleep.

The end.

THE TWO LITTLE PIGS

Two pigs lived in the forest.
One pig built a house out of straw.
He was lazy.
The other built a house out of stone.
He worked hard.
A hungry wolf came by and blew down the house made of straw.
The pigs hid in the stone house.
The wolf said, "Come out or I'll blow your house away."
But the pigs said, "No way."
The wolf blew and blew but couldn't do it.
He left the forest, and the pigs lived forever, together.

The end.
Time for bed.

SMALL GIRL, RED HOOD

Small girl
Red hood
Big wolf
In the woods.

Grandma's gone
Wolf in her cap
Girl at the door
Tap, tap.

Big ears to hear
Big eyes to see
Big teeth to eat
Girl better flee.

Strong woodsman
Just outside
Spied a wolf
Heard a girl's cries.

Axe swung
Wolf run
And the battle won
The woodsman said,
"Wow, I'm really tired, how about you?"

The end.

GOLDILOCKS AND THE BEARS

There were some bears;
It doesn't really matter how many.
There was a bunch.
Let's get to the point:
While they were out, a blond girl
Ate a bear's porridge,
Broke a bear's chair,
And fell asleep in a bear's bed.
When the bears came back,
They found her asleep.
She woke up, screamed, and ran home
So she could sleep in her own bed.
Just like you.

The end.

princess pea

Every young girl wanted to marry the prince.

To find a princess, the prince's mother put a pea
Under the mattress to see how each would sleep.

They all slept soundly, except one—she was so sensitive,
She had not slept well.

And so she married the prince.

Is there a pea under your bed?

Then what's your excuse?

Go to bed.

THE LITTLE RED HEN

None of the animals in the barnyard would help
The Little Red Hen plant or harvest or cook her vegetables.
"No, thanks," they said. "I don't wanna work."
But when the Little Red Hen's soup was ready, they said,
"Hey, I'll help you eat."
"No, thanks," said the hen.

The end.
Why are you still awake?

 ut in that peaceful little house
Atop the hill
On the other side of the woods...
Oh, you know where it is.
That fellow
With the kid
Who wouldn't go to sleep
Wasn't making much progress.

All these pigs, and bears,
And wolves, and chickens, and hens
Made such a racket that the child could not get to sleep.
And to make matters worse,
Someone got peas in the bed.

So the fellow picked up the pace,
Chopped stories in half.
No barnyard animals
Would get in his path.

DAVID AND GOLIATH

Goliath was a giant soldier with a sword.
David was a shepherd boy with a slingshot.
The two had a fight one night over who would be king.
David took careful aim with a stone
And knocked Goliath smack in the head.
The giant fell into a great heap.
He looked like he was asleep.

The end.

SLEEPING BEAUTY

A wicked fairy put a spell on a princess.
When she pricked her finger on a sewing machine,
Her entire family fell asleep for a hundred years.
Eventually a prince came along,
And finding the beautiful girl,
Gave her a kiss.
She woke, happy and refreshed
(and so did her parents).
Her advice to you:
Go to sleep!

The end.

Jack

Jack, be nimble
Jack, be quick
Jack, jump over the candlestick

Jack, close your eyes
Jack, not a peep
Jack, Jack, are you asleep?

Little Jack Horner
Sat in the corner,
Eating a blueberry pie.
He put in his thumb,
Pulled out a plum,
And . . . wait, Jack . . . I thought you were already asleep.

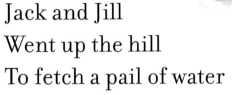

Jack and Jill
Went up the hill
To fetch a pail of water

Jack! What are you doing out of bed in the middle of the night?

HICKORY, DICKORY, DOCK

Hickory, dickory, dock,
A mouse ran up the clock.
The clock struck eight.
Oh, my, it's late!
So the mouse went straight to bed.

JOHN JACOB

John Jacob Jingleheimer Schmidt
His name is my name, too!
Whenever we go out,
The people always shout:
"John, John, get in bed and be quiet."

THE OLD LADY'S SHOE

There was an old lady
Who lived in a shoe.
She had so many kids,
She didn't know what to do.
Stories were read
Until her face turned blue.

When kids wouldn't go to bed,
She sold them to the zoo.

HEY DIDDLE DIDDLE

Hey diddle diddle, the cat and the fiddle.
The cow jumped over the moon.

If you don't fall asleep,
I'll run screaming from the room.

RIDDLE ONE

Why did the chicken cross the road?

To go to sleep.

RIDDLE TWO

Knock-knock.
Who's there?

Bed.
Bed who?

Bedder go to sleep.

nd they all lived...

THE END